BLEAK HOUSE

BLEAK HOUSE

Charles Dickens

Om KIDZ
An imprint of Om Books International

First published in 2018 by

Om Kidz | Om Books International

Corporate & Editorial Office
A-12, Sector 64, Noida 201 301
Uttar Pradesh, India
Phone: +91 120 477 4100
Email: editorial@ombooks.com
Website: www.ombooksinternational.com

Sales Office
107, Ansari Road, Darya Ganj
New Delhi 110 002, India
Phone: +91 11 4000 9000
Email: sales@ombooks.com
Website: www.ombooks.com

Adapted by Swayam Ganguly

ISBN: 978-93-85031-63-2

Printed in India

10 9 8 7 6 5 4 3 2 1

Contents

1.	The High Court of Chancery	7
2.	Progress Made	21
3.	Bleak House	45
4.	Richard's Profession	61
5.	My Past	81
6.	Lady Dedlock	97
7.	Richard's Decision	107
8.	The Breakup	115
9.	Mother Dear	127
10.	Jarndyce and Jarndyce	137
11.	The Secret	155
12.	The Letter and the Reply	161
13.	Enlightenment	173
14.	Perspective	187
15.	A Discovery	201
16.	An Upcoming Marriage	211
17.	Another Discovery	215
18.	Beginning a New World	227
About the Author		236
Characters		237
Questions		238

Chapter One

The High Court of Chancery

London. Lord Chancellor is seated in Lincoln's Inn Hall. A registrar is there below the judge, in wig and gown; and there are two or three maces, or petty-bags, or privy purses, or whatever one might choose to address them as, dressed in their legal court suits. All of them are yawning, as no crumb of amusement can ever be obtained from Jarndyce and Jarndyce, the cause in hand. This is because even the remote possibility of amusement was squeezed dry many, many years ago.

A little mad old woman is standing on a seat at the side of this hall, as this makes it convenient for her to peer into the curtained sanctuary and get a better glimpse of the events taking place there. This woman

is dressed in a rather squeezed bonnet and can always be counted to be present in court, right from the time the court sits till it rises. It is as if she is in perpetual expectation of some incomprehensible judgement that might be granted in her favour. Some are of the opinion that this woman is or was a party to a suit. But the truth is really this; no one knows this for certain because no one really cares! This little, mad woman carries some small litter in a reticule, calling them precious documents. But all these consist of mainly are dry lavender and paper matches really.

In the meantime, another man appears and it seems that his prospects in life have reached a conclusion. This man is one of the many ruined suitors and appears with periodical regularity from an area known as Shropshire. He breaks out in energetic efforts to address the Chancellor, just when the day's business has reached a conclusion. But sadly, this man can never be made to understand the simple fact that the Chancellor is legally ignorant of his very existence, after making it desolate for almost a quarter of a century. Undeterred, the man from

Shropshire still plants himself on a seat and is ready to call out, "My Lord!" in a voice that resembles the most sonorous complaint, no sooner than the judge rises from his seat.

Meanwhile, Jarndyce and Jarndyce drones on and on. This scarecrow of a suit has, in time, become so complicated that no man alive is able to grasp the details. The parties to it understand it least, but it has been noticed that no two Chancery lawyers are capable of talking about the case for five minutes without arriving at a total disagreement with regard to all its premises. Innumerable children have been born into the cause, just as innumerable young people have married into the cause as well. It is easy to conclude that innumerable old people have also died out of it.

There are many who have discovered themselves to be parties in Jarndyce and Jarndyce without any knowledge whatsoever as to how or why this happened. Likewise, several families have inherited legendary hatreds that this particular suit has brought about. That little plaintiff or defendant who was once promised a new rocking-horse, when Jarndyce and Jarndyce should be settled, has grown up, and is in possession of a real horse instead of a rocking-horse, galloped away into another world. The once fair wards of court have faded into either mothers or grandmothers and have settled into domesticity. Change has also been witnessed in the case of Chancellors, as the passage of time has witnessed a long procession of them making their entry and exiting from the court of law. The legion of bills in this suit have been transformed into mere bills of mortality.

Perhaps there are not three Jarndyces left upon this earth now, ever since old Tom Jarndyce decided to blow his brains out at a coffee-house in Chancery Lane. But despite this unfortunate suicide, the court suit of Jarndyce and Jarndyce drags on drearily, and in a manner that is both lengthy and perennially hopeless.

It would be a wide question if posed by someone as to how many people out of the suit Jarndyce and Jarndyce has spoiled and corrupted, by stretching forth its unwholesome hand. Thus, the Lord High Chancellor was seated in his High Court of Chancery now.

"Mr. Tangle," the Lord High Chancellor stated.

"Mlud," Mr. Tangle replied.

This man called Mr. Tangle knew more about Jarndyce and Jarndyce than any living soul. The man had achieved fame because of this knowledge. It was rumored that Mr. Tangle had never read anything else ever since he had left high school.

"Have you nearly concluded your argument, Mr. Tangle?" the Lord High Chancellor demanded.

"No, Mlud," Mr. Tangle replied quickly. "There are a variety of points that I feel are my duty to submit before you, my ludship."

"I believe several members of the bar are still to be heard?" the Chancellor stated, with the hint of a smile on his features. "We shall proceed with the hearing on Wednesday fortnight," he declared. Rising, he bowed to the bar and disappeared.

The rest of the people made themselves scarce quickly too. A battery of blue bags was loaded with heavy charges of papers and was carried off by clerks. The little mad woman also chose to vanish by marching away with

her precious documents and the now empty court was locked up. If only all the misery this court has caused, as well as the injustice it has committed, could be locked up with it, and the accumulation of the same could be burnt away in a big funeral pyre, it would serve the other parties better than the parties in Jarndyce and Jarndyce!

My Lady Dedlock has returned to her residence in town for a few days, prior to her departure to Paris. Her ladyship intends to stay there for a few weeks, and her movements are undecided after that. The childless My Lady Dedlock had been 'bored to death', quoting her own words, at her home in Lincolnshire, after her recent visit there.

Sir Leicester Dedlock is only a baronet but a mighty one. In fact, the mightiest one would not be an understatement. His family is as old as the hills and definitely more respectable. The baronet can be best described as an honourable, truthful, obstinate, greatly prejudiced, high-spirited, perfectly unreasonable man. Sir Leicester is twenty years older than his wife and married her for love.

An old-fashioned old gentleman called Mr. Tulkinghorn presented himself at her house in town. He is the attorney-at-law and eke solicitor of the High Court of Chancery and also has the honour of acting as the legal adviser of the Dedlocks. Sir Leicester Dedlock was happy to see Mr. Tulkinghorn.

"My Lady's cause has been again before the Chancellor, Mr. Tulkinghorn?" Sir Leicester enquired, offering his hand to his legal adviser.

"Yes, it has been on again today," he replied, with a quiet bow to My Lady. She was seated on a sofa beside the fire, shading her face with a hand-screen.

"Perhaps it would be useless to ask, whether anything has been done," she remarked, with the dreariness of Lincolnshire still upon her.

"Nothing that YOU would call as anything been done," Mr. Tulkinghorn replied.

"Nor ever will be," she stated.

"A few fresh affidavits have been placed upon the file," Mr. Tulkinghorn continued, "As these are short, I have proceeded to take trouble to beg leave, so I may possess my clients with any new proceedings in a cause."

Mr. Tulkinghorn was a cautious man, who took no more responsibility than necessary. "As you are headed for Paris, I have carried them in my pocket," he concluded.

Sir Leicester was accompanying his wife to Paris, but the latter was more delighted by the fashionable intelligence in the French capital. Mr. Tulkinghorn withdrew the papers, obtained permission to place them on a golden talisman of a table at My Lady's elbow, put on his spectacles and proceeded to read by the light of a shaded lamp.

Chapter Two

Progress Made

As I begin to write my portion of these pages, I face a great deal of difficulty. This is because I know I am not clever, and have always known this. I can well recall, when I was just a little girl, I used to address my doll when we were alone together this way, "Now, Dolly, you know very well that I am not clever, and so, you must be patient with me, like a dear!"

My doll used to sit in a great arm-chair, all propped up, staring at me, with her beautiful complexion and red, rosy lips. I think she stared at nothing rather than me actually while I stitched away busily and told her all my secrets. As far as I can recall, from my earliest memories,

I was raised just like a princess in a fairy story by my godmother. The only exception was that I was not quite the charming girl you would find in the fairy tales. My godmother was an exceptionally good woman, and if she had chosen to smile, she would have smiled just like an angel! She was a handsome woman, but alas, she never smiled. Instead, she was grave and strict. I think the evil that other people did made her frown all her life, and I was very sorry how unworthy I was of her, considering that she was such a good woman.

I spoke to my dear old doll quite a bit about this, and I think I never loved my godmother as much as I ought to have. It often crossed my mind that I would have been a much better girl, if only I had loved my godmother as she had deserved to be loved. This made me more timid and shy than I was naturally. Hence, Dolly was thrust upon me as the only friend around whom I was completely at ease. Then, something happened when I was still small, and this helped the cause. I had never heard my mama being spoken of and neither had I heard of my papa. I

was more interested in knowing about my mama though. But I had never been shown mama's grave and neither had I been told where it was. I had broached upon the subject to Mrs. Rachael, our only servant. "Esther, good night!" was her reply, and she had gone away, leaving me alone.

There were seven girls at the neighborhood school, where I was a day boarder and they called me little Esther Summerton. But I knew none of them at home, and there were holidays at school on other birthdays, but none on mine. From what I had overheard at school, the other girls had birthday celebrations at home, but there were none on my birthday! My birthday was the most melancholy day for me at home in the entire year. I am known to be a very affectionate girl, and I still felt the wound even though it was only for a day. "It would have been far better, Esther, if you did not have a birthday at all," my godmother stated gloomily after dinner on my birthday. "It would have been better had you never been born."

I broke out in tears. "Oh, dear godmother, pray tell me, did Mama die on my birthday?"

"No," she replied. "Ask me no more, child!"

"Oh, pray tell me something about her," I pleaded, sobbing. "What did I do to mama? Why is it my fault? No, no, dear godmother, don't go away. Oh, speak to me!" My fright had exceeded my sorrow now, and I knelt as I caught hold of her dress. "Let me go!" she had been insisting all this while, but now she stood still. She raised me and sat down in her chair. She made me stand before her and declared in a low, cold voice, "Esther, your mother is your disgrace, just as you are hers. I have forgiven her and the wrong she did to me," she said relentlessly. "I say no more of it. Now, go!"

I went up to my room and cried myself to sleep that night, with my doll's cheek against mine wet with tears. I slept that night clutching my solitary friend upon my bosom. I felt the distance between me and my godmother widen much more after my birthday. I felt so guilty of filling up a place in her house that actually should have been empty that I did not find her approachable after that.

One sunny afternoon, I had returned home from school as usual and was gliding up the stairs to my room. My godmother called me back after peeping out of the parlour-door. I discovered a stranger seated with her which was rather unusual. "This," she said in an undertone, "is the child." Then, she added in that typical stern manner of hers, "This is Esther, sir."

The gentleman scrutinized me by putting up his eye-glasses. "Come here, my dear," he said. He shook hands with me, asking me to take off my bonnet, staring at me all the time. "Ah!" he stated, after I had done so, and "Yes!" afterwards. Then, he nodded to my godmother. "You may go upstairs, Esther," she stated. I made the gentleman my curtsy and left.

Almost two years later, when I was almost fourteen, my godmother fell down on the floor one dreadful night. There was no need for me to cry out, as her voice had resonated throughout the house and had even been heard on the street. She lay on her bed for more than a week after that. The day after my poor godmother was buried, that gentleman arrived again.

"My name is Kenge," he stated. "Kenge and Carboy, Lincoln's Inn. Have you ever heard of Jarndyce and Jarndyce?"

"Never!" I replied.

"Well, Mr. Jarndyce, aware of your desolate position, makes an offer to place you at a first-rate establishment, where your education can be completed and comfort can be secured. Now, what does our young friend have to say to that?" he enquired. "Take your time! I shall wait for your reply."

This interview took place at Windsor, where I had passed my whole life so far. But now, I left Windsor on the stagecoach for Reading. I am ashamed to admit that I had wrapped my dear old doll in her own shawl and buried her in the garden-earth under the tree shading my old window. I carried my bird in his cage, and he was my sole companion. "Miss Donny," a rather neat lady looked up at my window and declared when the stagecoach halted at Reading.

"No, ma'am, Esther Summerson," I replied. "That is quite right. Miss Donny," the lady stated, and I realized now that she was introducing herself. A neat maid directed my boxes to a small green carriage that was driven away after Miss Donny, the maid and I alighted it. "Everything has been made ready for you, Esther," Miss Donny declared. "The scheme of your pursuits has been arranged in exact accordance with the wishes of your guardian, Mr. Jarndyce."

"Do you know Mr. Jarndyce, ma'am?" I asked.

"Not personally, Esther. Merely through his solicitors, Messrs. Kenge and Carboy, of London. Mr. Kenge is a very superior gentleman and truly eloquent indeed."

My confusion only deepened at our speedy arrival at our destination, and I shall never forget how uncertain and unreal everything was that afternoon at Greenleaf, Miss Donny's house. But I adapted quickly to Greenleaf, and nothing could have been more orderly and precise. I passed six quiet years there. One November morning, I received this letter.

Old Square, Lincoln's Inn

To Miss Esther Summerson

Madam,

Our client Mr. Jarndyce being about to receive into his house, under an Order of the Ct of Chy, a Ward of the Ct in this cause, for whom he wishes to secure an eligible companion. He directs us to inform you that he will be glad of your services in the aforesaid capacity.

We have arranged for your being forwarded, carriage free, eight o'clock coach from Reading, next Monday morning, to White Horse Cellar, Piccadilly, London, where one of our clerks will be in waiting for you.

We are, Madam, Your obedient servants,

Kenge and Carboy

I shall never ever forget the emotion caused in the house thanks to this letter that gave just five days' notice for my removal. I received evidence of the love and kindness that existed in that house for me each minute of those last five days. Everyone was sad that I was leaving. I was surrounded and showered with parting presents.

I thanked each one of them from the bottom of my heart, including Miss Donny and all the maids. I was overwhelmed when the maids said, "Bless you, miss, wherever you go!" and when the lame, old gardener, who I thought barely noticed me all these years, came running after the coach, puffing and panting, to hand me a little nosegay of geraniums. He told me that I had been the light of his eyes! I decided that I should not cry after so much had been done for me. So, I cheered myself up, cooling my eyes with lavender water.

We reached London and I was received by a young gentleman who led me to Mr. Kenge's office. He hadn't changed a bit but was surprised and pleased to find me so altered. "Miss Summerson, as you are going to be the companion of the young lady who is present now in the Chancellor's private room, we thought you should be in attendance as well," he declared and led me by the arm to a comfortable room. A young lady and a young gentleman stood beside a big, loud-roaring fire. They looked up when I entered, and the young lady was radiantly beautiful with

rich golden hair, soft blue eyes and a bright, innocent, trusting face. "Miss Ada," Mr. Kenge said. "This is Miss Summerson."

The lady approached me with her hands extended, and with a smile of welcome. She appeared to change her mind in an instant and kissed me instead. She was naturally blessed with a captivating and winning personality. We were seated in the window-seat in a few minutes, talking warmly and freely, enjoying the warmth of the fire. The young gentleman was her distant cousin and his name was Richard Carstone. He was a handsome young man, with an engaging laugh. He joined us and spoke freely like a light-hearted boy. He could not be more than nineteen but was almost two years older than her. What was unusual was that they had met for the first time that day as well.

It was surely unusual for the three of us to come together for the first time in such an unusual place. It was a subject worthy of conversation, but we conversed in a low tone because a full-dressed gentleman in a bag

wig frequently entered and exited the room. He informed Mr. Kenge that the Chancellor would be with us in five minutes. Presently, we heard the bustle and a tread of feet, and Mr. Kenge announced that the Court had risen and his lordship was in the adjoining room.

The gentleman in the bag wig opened the door and requested Mr. Kenge to enter. All of us entered the next room and saw his lordship seated in an arm-chair at a table near the fire, dressed in plain black. He gave us a searching look, but his manner was kind and courtly.

"Miss Ada Clare?" the Lord Chancellor enquired, and Mr. Kenge presented her. His lordship requested Ada to sit next to him.

"The Jarndyce in question, is Jarndyce of Bleak House," the Lord Chancellor said, turning over leaves.

"Yes, my lord," Mr. Kenge replied. "In Hertfordshire," he added.

"He is not married?" his lordship enquired.

"He is not, my lord."

"Is young Mr. Richard Carstone present?"

Richard bowed, stepping forward.

"Mr. Jarndyce of Bleak House, my lord, if I may remind your lordship, provides a suitable companion for Miss Ada Clare. This is the young lady. Miss Summerson," Mr. Kenge announced.

"Miss Summerson is not related to any party in the cause, I think?"

"No, my lord."

He dismissed us in a pleasant manner and we exited. An open carriage arrived for us at one o'clock, as well as a cart for our luggage.

Chapter Three

Bleak House

As we headed westward, the day brightened. We entered the suburbs and got on a country road again. Windmills, rick-yards, milestones, farmer's wagons, scents of old hay, swinging signs and horse troughs greeted our eyes. Trees, fields, and hedge rows dotted the countryside. The green landscape was delightful to behold.

"That's Bleak House!" the driver declared, pointing with his whip towards a light sparkling on the top of a hill before us. He urged his horses into a canter, and we travelled so fast, uphill though it was, that the wheels dispatched road drift that flew about our heads, just like spray from a water-mill.

It appeared to be an old-fashioned house, with three peaks in the front roof and a circular sweep that led to the porch. We heard a bell as we drew up, and dogs barking in the distance. A gush of light emerged from the open door, and the smoking and steaming of the heated horses merged with the quickened beating of our own hearts, as we alighted in considerable confusion.

"Ada, my love, Esther, my dear, welcome! I rejoice to see you all! Rick, if only I had a hand to spare at the moment, I would gladly give it to you," a gentleman declared hospitably, as he held me and Ada by the waist, kissing us in a fatherly way. He guided us across the hall into a small, cozy room, glowing with a blazing fire.

"Now, Rick!" he exclaimed, after we were seated on a sofa by the hearth. "I have a hand at liberty now! An earnest word is as good as speech! I am glad to see you. Warm yourself! You are at home!"

Richard shook him by both hands, gratefully and respectfully. "You are very kind, sir! We are very much obliged to you."

"How did you like the ride, my dear?" Mr. Jarndyce

enquired of Ada. I saw that he had a handsome, lively face and had silvered iron-grey hair. He appeared to be nearing sixty than fifty, but was hearty, energetic and robust.
"Come, girls, come and see your new home!" he said invitingly. The house was one of those delightfully irregular ones that lead you up and down steps, out of one room and into another. You come across more rooms when you think you have witnessed them all, and there is a bountiful provision of small halls and passages. Still, you discover older cottage-rooms in places least expected, with lattice windows and green growth peeking through them.

Our luggage had arrived, and I was dressed when a maid fetched a basket into my room with two bunches of labelled keys in it.

"For you, miss, if you please," she said.

"For me?" I asked.

"The housekeeping keys, miss."

I displayed surprise, and she added with some surprise as well, "I was instructed to bring them as soon as you were alone, miss. Miss Summerson, if I don't deceive myself?"

"Yes."

"The large bunch is the housekeeping and the small one is the cellars, miss."

I said I would be ready at half-past six when she asked me for a time to show me the presses and things they belonged to. Ada arrived and I showed her the keys. She had such a delightful confidence in me that I felt that it would be insensibility and ingratitude on my part not to feel encouraged at my responsibilities. I had no problems with my two bunches of keys later, as each part of the house was in perfect order. I was so busy the next day that I could not believe it was breakfast time already when I heard the bell ring.

As I passed through the passages, Mr. Jarndyce summoned me into a small room next to his bed-chamber. "Sit down, my dear. This is the growlery. I come and growl here when I am out of humour."

"You must be here very seldom, sir," I replied.

"Oh, you don't know me," he declared. "The growlery is the most used room in the house. You are not aware of half my humours yet. How you tremble, my dear!"

I could not help it! I tried my best, but alone in his benevolent presence, meeting his kind eyes, and feeling so happy and honoured by him—I kissed his hand. I don't remember what I said to him or even if I spoke at all. He walked to the window in a disconcerted manner, and it almost appeared that he wanted to jump out. Then, he turned, and I was reassured to see in his eyes that he had gone there merely to hide. I sat down when he gently patted me on the head.

"There! There! That's over. Pooh! Don't be foolish," he stated.

"It won't happen again, sir," I replied. "At first, it is not easy..."

"Nonsense!" he exclaimed. "It is easy! Why is it not? I hear of a good old orphan girl without a protector, and I decide to be her protector. She grows up, justifying my good decision, and I decide to remain her guardian and friend. There is nothing in it!"

Mr. Jarndyce began speaking with me as confidentially as if he did so every morning. I almost felt he did so.

"You don't understand this Chancery business, do you Esther?" he asked, and I shook my head.

"I don't know who does. The lawyers have twisted it into such a state of bedevilment that the original merits of the case have fast disappeared. It is about a will and the trusts under it. But now, it's nothing but costs. We are always appearing, disappearing, interrogating, filing, cross-filing, arguing, sealing, and motioning, referring, reporting, and revolving about the Lord Chancellor and all his satellites. We are waltzing away to a dusty death in terms of costs. The rest has faded away by some extraordinary means," he raved and then paused to rub his head.

"It was about a will, sir?" I probed to bring him back.

"Yes. A certain Jarndyce made a great fortune in an evil hour," he disclosed. "He made a great will and the fortune left behind by the will is squandered away. The legatees under the will are reduced to such miserable circumstances that they would be punished if they had committed a great crime in having money left them. The will itself is made a dead letter, and we can't get out of the suit either, even after so many years. This is because

we have been made parties to it, and MUST BE parties to it, irrespective of the fact that we like it or not. My great uncle, poor Tom Jarndyce, began thinking of it, and it was the beginning of the end. This was his house, Esther, and I was his heir. It was bleak indeed when I arrived here, as he had left the signs of his misery upon the house. But, to return to our gossip. Here's Rick, a fine, young, promising fellow. What's to be done with him?"

"Oh my goodness!" I thought. "The idea of asking my advice on such a matter!"

"Here he is, Esther," Mr. Jarndyce announced. "He must have a profession and must make a choice himself. My dear, he is a ward at Chancery. Kenge and Carboy will have something to say about it. So will counsel and the Chancellor."

"Perhaps, it would be best to ask Mr. Richard about what he intends to do," I offered.

"Exactly," he replied. "That is what I mean, dear. You can talk it over with him and Ada, using your tact and quiet ways. See what you make of it. We will surely arrive at the heart of the matter by your means, little woman!"

I replied that I would try my best, although I feared he gave me more credit than what was due. I felt that it was required to voice this, but he only laughed pleasantly when I did.

"I think we have done enough with the growlery for one day," he declared, pushing back his chair and rising. He took my arm and we went in search of Ada. From that hour onwards, I was quite at ease with him. I was quite unreserved, content in whatever little I knew and very happy.

Chapter Four

Richard's Profession

Ada and I read together, worked, and spent our time in such gainful employment that the winter flew by us like bright-winged birds. Richard accompanied us normally in the afternoons and always in the evenings. He was one of the most restless creatures, but was very fond of our company. He was especially fond of Ada, and although I have never witnessed young people falling in love before, I found them out pretty soon. I cannot say that I knew everything about it, of course, and I did ask myself if I was growing deceitful by nature.

I was always quiet as a mouse anyway, and so were they as far as the spoken word was concerned as a form of expressing love. But the innocent way that they relied

upon me as they took to one another more and more, was charming to say the least. I had to conceal my interest with great difficulty.

After many discussions about Richard's profession, initially without Mr. Jarndyce, and later with him, progress on the matter was achieved. Richard stated he was ready for anything, and while Mr. Jarndyce cast his doubts about his being too old to enter the Navy, Richard agreed. Mr. Jarndyce asked Richard his opinion of the Army and received the reply that it wasn't a bad idea. Mr. Jarndyce asked Richard if his preference for the sea was a natural boyish inclination or a strong passion, Richard replied that he wasn't sure.

"I haven't the slightest idea of what I'd be," a confused Richard confessed. "I'm certain I don't want to go into the Church, though."

"Do you want to follow in Mr. Kenge's footsteps?" Mr. Jarndyce asked.

"I don't know about that, sir!" Richard replied. "I'm fond of boating though, and articled clerks travel a good deal on the water. It's a capital profession!"

"Surgeon?" Mr. Jarndyce offered.

"That's the thing, sir!" Richard exclaimed enthusiastically. "We have got it at last. M.R.C.S.!"

I doubt if Richard had ever thought of it once before. But Richard could not be laughed at as he stated that he had chosen his profession, and his destiny was the art of healing. I think he was simply enamored by the latest idea and was happy to get rid of the problem of choosing a profession.

Mr. Jarndyce went out of his way to discuss this matter with Richard with the utmost seriousnes and to impose upon him not to treat this issue in a light hearted manner. Richard appeared serious after these interviews, but eventually assured me and Ada that all was well and began speaking about something else. It was considered sensible to take Mr. Kenge into council. He arrived at dinner one day and did exactly what he had done with me when I was a little girl.

"Ah!" he said, turning his eye-glasses over and over. "Yes, a very good profession indeed, Mr. Jarndyce."

"The course of study and preparing for it requires diligent

pursuit," my guardian observed, looking at Richard.

"No doubt," Mr. Kenge replied. "Diligently."

Richard said he would do his best and Mr. Kenge stated that Richard should be placed with some eminent practitioner to begin with.

"I think that can be easily arranged, Mr. Jarndyce," Mr. Kenge stated. "After we identify a suitable practitioner, we should add our ability to pay a premium. The only difficulty would be the selection of one person from such a large number. It might be a coincidence that I happen to have a cousin in the medical profession named Bayham Badger. He might appear eligible to you, and MIGHT respond to your proposal."

It was decided that Mr. Kenge would meet his cousin regarding the matter, and our visit to London as proposed by Mr. Jarndyce was combined with Richard's business. London was a great wonder for us, and we took up lodgings at a cheerful place near Oxford Street, over an upholsterer's shop. We were outdoors sightseeing for hours on end. We had a dinner invitation at Mr. Badger's residence, the day matters came to a conclusion

about Mr. Badger and Richard. We arrived and met Mrs. Badger, who was about fifty but youthfully dressed and of a fine complexion. Mr. Bayham Badger was a pink, fresh-faced, crisp-looking gentleman with light hair and white teeth. He had a weak voice and his eyes looked surprised. He looked a few years younger than Mrs. Badger to me. Dinner was handsomely served, and it was a very genteel entertainment. A gentleman called Mr. Woodcourt was also invited to this dinner party. He was a dark complexioned young surgeon. Although he was rather reserved, I found him sensible and agreeable. At least, I said yes when Ada asked me if I did.

I observed that evening that Ada and Richard were even strongly attached in each other's company. This was but natural, as they were about to be separated so soon. Therefore, I was not surprised when Ada was unusually silent after we had reached home. But I was taken unawares when she came into my arms, and spoke to me with her face hidden. "I have a great secret to tell you, darling Esther," she whispered.

"What is it, Ada?"

"Oh, Esther, you'd never guess!"

"Shall I try?"

"No! Please don't!" Ada exclaimed, startled at the thought.

"Now then, I wonder who it can be about?" I said, pretending to think.

"It's about my cousin, Richard," Ada whispered.

"What about him?"

"He says, I know it sounds foolish as we are both so young," Ada said, and immediately burst into tears. "He says he loves me dearly, Esther."

"Does he now?" I stated in jest. "I've never heard of such a thing! Why, my pet, I could have told you that many weeks ago!"

Ada lifted up her head in joyful surprise, and held me round the neck. She cried, blushed and laughed, and it was pleasant to see.

"You must take me for an absolute goose, darling," I stated. "Richard has been in love with you for I don't know how long."

"But you never spoke a word about it," Ada exclaimed, kissing me.

"I waited to be told, dear," I replied.

"You don't think it's wrong, do you?"

"But you don't mean to say that you...?" I began jokingly, and Ada broke out in sobs. "Yes, I do! You know I do! With my whole heart, Esther!"

I told Ada laughingly now that I had known that as well. We sat beside the fire, and I spoke to her. She was soon happy, and left after I promised to speak to our guardian about it.

"Guardian," I said to Mr. Jarndyce, the next day. "Ada and Richard have fallen in love!"

"Already?" Mr. Jarndyce cried, quite astonished.

"Yes. To tell you the truth, I had expected it to happen."

"The deuce you did!" he exclaimed. He smiled, and sat considering the matter for a while, and asked to see them. He held Ada in a fatherly way when they arrived, and addressed Richard cheerfully, "Rick, I am glad to have won your confidence, and hope to preserve it. The relations between the four of us have brightened up my life considerably, and new interests and pleasures have kindled it. I had contemplated the possibility of you and

your cousin going through life together, and I find it totally desirable. But that was afar off, Rick."

"We look afar off, sir," Richard replied.

"Well, that's rational," Mr. Jarndyce stated. "Now, I might tell you that you two don't know your own minds yet and that plenty of things might divert you from each other. I could tell you that the chain of flowers you have created might easily become a chain of lead. But I shall refrain from saying that as such wisdom will come soon to you, and naturally, if I daresay, it will come at all. I will assume, hopefully, that you will be in each other's hearts the same way after a few years, as you are now. But if you DO change, if you DO find that you are commonplace cousins as a man and woman, than you were as boy and girl, do not be ashamed to confide in me. There will be nothing monstrously wrong or uncommon in it as I am only your friend and kinsman. I have no power over you, and only hope to retain your confidence."

"I am sure I speak for Ada as well, sir, when I say that you have the strongest power over us both," Richard stated. "We have the greatest respect, gratitude and love for you that only strengthens each day."

"Dear cousin John," Ada added, "My father's place can never be empty again, and all the love and duty I could have rendered to him is now transferred to you."

"Let us look hopefully at the future," Mr. Jarndyce declared. "Rick, the world is before you, and is ready to receive you. Trust only in providence and your own efforts, and like the heathen waggoner, never separate the two. Constancy in love is good, but means nothing, and is nothing without constancy in every kind of effort. Even if you were blessed with the abilities of all great men, you wouldn't be able to do anything well if you did not sincerely mean it and set about it. If you nurse the idea that any real success can be wrested from fortune by fits and starts, either abandon that notion right here, or abandon your cousin Ada here."

"I will leave IT here, sir," Richard replied, smiling. "If I did bring it here, and I hope I did not though. I will work my way on to my cousin Ada in that hopeful future."

"Yes," Mr. Jarndyce said. "Why should you pursue her if you are not to make her happy?"

"I wouldn't make her unhappy, even for my love,"

Richard declared proudly. "Well said," Mr. Jarndyce exclaimed. "She will remain here, in her home with me. Love her, Rick in your active life, as well as when you return home, and all will be well. Otherwise, all will go ill. I will stop my preaching now. I think you and Ada should take a walk now."

Ada embraced Mr. Jarndyce tenderly, and Richard shook his hand heartily. Then, the lovers exited the room together.

Chapter Five

My Past

Richard departed the very next day to embark on his new career and entrusted Ada to my charge with great trust. It touched me then, and it touches me now, to think that they both thought of me in those hard times. I was included in all their plans, present or future. I was supposed to write to Richard once a week, reporting about Ada, who would write to Richard every alternate day. I was to be informed by Richard about all his labours and successes, and I was supposed to be Ada's bridesmaid when they were married. I was also supposed to live with them after that and to keep the keys to their house.

"The suit might make us rich, Esther," Richard stated, to crown it all, and a shade crossed Ada's face.

"Why not, my dearest Ada?" Richard asked.

"It might as well declare us poor at once," Ada stated.

"Oh, I don't know about that. But under any circumstance, it won't declare anything at once. It hasn't done so in god knows how many years."

"True," Ada offered.

"But the longer it goes on, the nearer it must be to a settlement. Isn't that reasonable?" Richard reasoned.

"I'm afraid, Richard, that it will make us unhappy if we trust it," Ada stated.

"But, my dear Ada, we are not going to trust to it," Richard exclaimed. "It SHOULD just make us rich. The court is supposed to give us what is rightfully ours, and it's not needed to quarrel with right."

"No, but it might be better to forget about it."

"Then we shall forget about it and consign the entire thing to oblivion."

But although Richard said he wanted to end it, he continued building as many castles in the air as the number of men that built the Great Wall of China. Richard left in high spirits, and although Ada and I would miss him very much, we focused on our quieter career.

Richard came to see us often when we were in London, and always delighted with his great spirits and freshness. But although I was very fond of him, I regretted that he lacked application and concentration.

One day, Mr. and Mrs. Bayham Badger came home when my guardian was away. As I conversed with them, I inquired after Richard.

"Mr. Carstone is very well," Mrs. Badger replied. "He is a great acquisition to our society. But I...you won't consider me premature if I mention something?"

I said no, but I found Mrs. Badger's tone rather insinuating.

"Miss Clare?" Mrs. Badger asked sweetly, and Ada said no too, although she looked uneasy.

"My dears, I feel Mr. Carstone hasn't chosen his profession wisely."

Ada looked rather anxious, so I asked Mrs. Badger how she had arrived at this supposition.

"Mr. Carstone's character and conduct prove that," Mrs. Badger replied. "His easy disposition makes him suppress his true feelings, but it's obvious that he feels languid about the profession. He lacks that positive interest that's needed to make it his vocation."

"Does Mr. Badger think the same?" Ada enquired.

"Well, to be honest, Miss Clare," Mr. Badger declared, "The matter had not crossed my mind until Mrs. Badger mentioned it. But I have arrived at the same conclusion as Mrs. Badger."

Both Ada and I felt that the probability of their opinion being sound was great. We decided not to speak to Mr. Jarndyce unless we had spoken to Richard first, as he was returning the next evening. When Richard arrived, and I questioned him, he said he did not care much about the profession, but it would serve just as well as anything else. I told him to be serious about his chosen profession, and he became grave. "I've been thinking," Richard declared. "I think the law is my boy."

"The law!" Ada repeated.

"I would be able to study and master it if I went into Kenge's office," Richard thought aloud, and I thought it best to provide him encouragement under the circumstances.

Ada and I requested Richard to be open and frank with Mr. Jarndyce, and when our guardian heard what Richard heard to say, he told him to retreat with honour,

but commit no more mistakes for his cousin Ada's sake. "Look before you leap and take a lot of time about it," Mr. Jarndyce advised. Richard was so energetic that he wanted to step into Mr. Kenge's office that very moment, but he resigned to our caution.

"Cousin John, you don't think the worse of Richard, I hope?" Ada asked our guardian, after Richard had left.

"No, my love," he replied.

"It is natural and common to be mistaken like that," Ada reasoned.

"Don't look so unhappy, Ada dear."

"I am not unhappy, Cousin John," Ada smiled cheerfully, and said. "But I would be if you thought worse of Richard."

"My dear, I'd only think worse of him if he made you unhappy. I'd quarrel with myself rather than with Rick, as I was the one who brought the two of you together. All this is nothing, as he has time before him and can run the race."

Mr. Jarndyce bade us goodnight, but I could barely sleep. So, I engaged myself in some ornamental work. I had left some silk downstairs in a work-table drawer

in that room that served as the growlery. I went to fetch it with a candle and was surprised to see my guardian sitting in the room. He was absorbed in thought, and started when he saw me. "Esther!"

"At work so late?" he enquired, when I told him what I'd come for.

"I couldn't sleep. But you look tired and are late too, dear guardian. I hope no trouble keeps you awake?"

"None that YOU would readily understand, little woman," he replied in a tone so regretful that I repeated his words automatically. He urged me to stay for a while as I was in his thoughts. "I hope I am not the trouble, guardian?" I asked.

"I think, little woman, that you need to know of your own history. Whatever I know is very little though."

"If you think so, guardian."

"Nine years have passed, my dear, since I received a letter from a lady living in isolation. The letter informed me of a girl child, a twelve-year-old orphan. The writer had raised her secretly since her birth after obliterating all traces of her existence. If the writer died before this child became a woman, she would be left totally friendless and

nameless. The writer urged and requested me to finish her incomplete work. I was concerned and replied to the letter."

I took my guardian's hand and kissed it in gratitude. "The lady said she was the child's aunt. My dear, that's all I know," Mr. Jarndyce concluded, as I held his hand. "I always knew my ward was useful, beloved, and happy as I saw her more than she saw me. She repays me twenty thousandfold, and twenty more, every hour, every day." "She blesses the guardian who is a father to her, oftener still," I replied. He seemed troubled at the word father, but he subdued the feeling. But I had noticed it, and I felt my words had shocked him. "Take a fatherly good night, and rest, my dear," he said, kissing me on the forehead. I did not think or work that night, but thanked the heavens for its kindness, and fell asleep.

Richard making a trial at Mr. Kenge's office was not as easy as it had appeared. He began to doubt the sanity of leaving Mr. Badger now. He said he wasn't sure. It wasn't a bad profession, and he supposed he could give it another chance as maybe he liked it as well as any other profession.

He locked himself up with some books to acquire a great deal of information rapidly. This fervor lasted for a month before it began to cool and then it warmed again. This tug-of-war between medicine and law lasted so long that it was midsummer before Richard finally separated from Mr. Badger, to enter an experimental course of Messrs. Kenge and Carboy. Richard appeared so high-spirited, earnest and so in love with Ada, that it was difficult not to be pleased with him.

Chapter Six

Lady Dedlock

We went for a walk to the little church in the park on Sunday morning. The congregation at the church was very small and a rustic one with the exception of a large number of servants from the house. I observed that the church smelt earthy like a grave and was an ancient, solemn, shady little church.

But my heart beat wildly, as I saw her! Those handsome, haughty eyes met mine, and locked. A moment later, I cast my eyes down on my book. But I knew that beautiful face well. Strangely, I had never seen the lady ever in my life, but the flutter in my heart was caused the association of that face with my early life at my

godmother's house. I learnt easily that the gouty, grey-haired gentleman, who was the only other occupant of that great pew, was Sir Leicester Dedlock. The woman was Lady Dedlock, but I was unaware why her face triggered old memories in my mind and a wild beating of my heart.

Did my godmother's face really resemble that of Lady Dedlock? It could be, but the expressions were certainly different on the two faces. Lady Dedlock did not look stern like my godmother, but I had never seen such haughtiness and loftiness as reflected on Lady Dedlock's face. I, Esther Summerson, was evoked out of the past by some strange power this fashionable lady possessed; a lady I was sure I had never set eyes upon before this. I slowly stopped trembling and conquered this strange emotion. I stared at Lady Dedlock again and my heart did not beat wildly. She did not pay me any heed, but looked at Ada and me once or twice through her glass. After the service concluded, Sir Leicester escorted Lady Dedlock out of the church, and I noticed he walked with the aid of a walking stick.

The week trudged on to Saturday, and Mr. Jarndyce, Ada and I were seated at our favourite spot in the woods. We liked watching nature's beauties, the birds, and insects here. Suddenly, we heard thunder and soon large raindrops burst through the leaves. We ran to take shelter in a lodge nearby. The lodge was dark and the sky overcast. A man appeared at the door to place two chairs for Ada and me.

As we watched the storm, the strange beating of my heart returned. Lady Dedlock emerged from within the lodge and stood behind my chair. She had taken shelter in that lodge before we had arrived. "Have I frightened you?" she asked.

"No! Why should I be frightened?" I replied.

"I believe I have the pleasure of addressing Mr. Jarndyce," Lady Dedlock said to my guardian.

"Your remembrance does me more honour, than I supposed it would, Lady Dedlock," he replied.

She spoke to him pleasantly yet indifferently. She was beautiful, elegant, self-possessed and could attract

anyone's attention. The keeper fetched her a chair and she sat between us. It seemed that she respected Mr. Jarndyce and even wished to appease him.

"I presume this is your other ward, Miss Clare?"

Mr. Jarndyce presented Ada to Lady Dedlock.

"Present me," she turned towards me, "to this young lady too!"

"Miss Summerson is also my ward," Mr. Jarndyce stated.

"She is fortunate to have such a guardian!"

I replied to Lady Dedlock that I was indeed, and she instantly turned away from me hastily.

"I think you were more acquainted with my sister than me," she said to him over her shoulder.

"Yes, we met oftener," Mr. Jarndyce replied.

"We went separate ways," Lady Dedlock stated. "But we had little in common even before we decided to differ."

The storm was over, and the shower had abated. We spotted a little pony phaeton approach.

"The messenger returns with the carriage, my Lady," the keeper announced.

"I am sorry that we are not likely to renew our former

acquaintance," Lady Dedlock said to Mr. Jarndyce, and asked him to allow her to send the carriage back for his two wards. Mr. Jarndyce declined this offer, and she took a graceful leave of Ada, ignoring me, as she stepped into the carriage.

Chapter Seven

Richard's Decision

We saw no more of Lady Dedlock after that, except at church on Sundays. Her face evoked the same feelings in me, and I was unaware if the experience was painful or pleasurable, whether it attracted me or made me despise her. I admired her with some fear, and in her presence, my mind wandered back to my childhood days.

Richard was constant in his visits. Besides coming every weekend, he would sometimes ride up on horseback, to spend the evening with us, and ride back early next day. Although he assured us he was very industrious, I could not be assured. He told us he had got to the core of the mystery of the suit now and that only made me more worried. The suit had caused nothing but sorrow and ruin,

and it stuck to Richard like some kind of infatuation. He had even begun to haunt the court.

Ada was blinded in love to mistrust Richard's thoughts and actions, and Mr. Jarndyce chose to maintain a stony silence on the matter. So, I decided to have a little chat with Richard one day.

"Are you beginning to feel settled, now, Richard?" I asked him, as we walked arm in arm.

"Yes, my dear," he replied. "I'm all right."

"Settled?"

"What do you mean, settled?"

"Settled in the law, Richard."

"Oh, yes."

"You said that before, dear Richard."

"Settled as in settling down, you mean?" Richard enquired.

"Yes."

"Well, I can't say I'm settling down," he replied. "One can't settle down as this business itself is in such an unsettled state. I mean the forbidden subject when I say business, of course."

"Do you think it will ever reach a settled state?"

"Undoubtedly," Richard replied.

We walked for a while without speaking and then Richard spoke to me frankly, "Dear Esther, I should have held on to Badger or Kenge and Carboy for dear life, and would have been steady and systematic by now, and not in debt, and..."

"ARE you in debt, Richard?" I exclaimed.

"Yes, I am a little, dear," Richard confessed. "You hate me, Esther, don't you?"

"You know I don't, Richard."

"You are kinder to me than myself," Richard stated. "I know I am an unfortunate dog not to be more settled, Esther. But how CAN I? After the final hearing, we shall get judgment in our favour. Then, you and Ada shall see what I can be! I have been studying the papers deeply for months. We shall emerge triumphant! I have had enough of working at Jarndyce and Jarndyce like a galley slave. I have no liking for the law, and it unsettles me even more. It's not as if I desired a profession for life anyway. I shall be well provided for when the proceedings are terminated. Then, I can pursue the profession that suits me. What could it be?" he asked, and I shook my head.

"The army, of course," Richard stated with perfect conviction.

"The army?" I blabbered.

Richard displayed the calculations he had made in his pocket-book. Suppose, he told me, he had contracted two hundred pounds of debt in six months out of the army; and contracted no debt at all within a corresponding period in the army, this step involved a saving of four hundred pounds a year, or two thousand pounds in five years. This was a large sum, indeed, and the way he spoke about distancing himself from Ada to repay her love and to provide for her happiness by conquering all odds, made my heart ache.

I spoke to Richard earnestly and pleaded with him for Ada's sake, not to rest any hopes on the Chancery. Richard agreed to whatever I said, in his easy going manner. Alas! When would that dreaded suit loosen its hold over him? We had a lengthy conversation, but talk about the suit still returned to feature in our conversation.

Chapter Eight

The Breakup

Richard communicated what he had in mind to Mr. Jarndyce. I'm doubtful if my guardian was surprised, but it did cause him much disappointment and uneasiness. He was often closeted together with Richard, late night and early morning. They passed entire days in London together, had several appointments with Mr. Kenge, working their way through disagreeable business. We learnt later, that a new application had been made to the Lord Chancellor on Richard's behalf, as an infant and a ward. I don't know the details, but there was a lot of talk regarding this. The Lord Chancellor described him in

open court as an annoying and fickle infant. I heard that the matter had been adjourned, readjourned, referred, reported on, and petitioned, till Richard joked that if he entered the army at all, it might be when he was seventy years old.

Finally, an appointment was secured for Richard to meet the Lord Chancellor in his private room. The latter chided Richard for trifling with time, and not knowing his mind. Richard thought it was a good joke coming from the Lord Chancellor, but finally his request was granted. His name found entry at the Horse Guards as an applicant for an ensign's commission. The purchase money was deposited with an agent, and Richard, rather characteristically, dived headlong into a violent course of military study. He even woke up at five o'clock to practice the broadsword technique. Richard visited us less frequently now that he was in London. Time went by, and he finally received the commission with orders to join a regiment in Ireland. He arrived to have a

lengthy discussion with my guardian. Mr. Jarndyce soon summoned me and Ada into the room. He told Ada that he and Richard had had a difference of opinion. "You are hard on me, sir," Richard stated. "It is harder as you have been considerate in all aspects and been so kind to me than I can ever expect. But I think I am the best judge for myself."

"I hope you excuse me when I say this, dear Rick," Mr. Jarndyce said cheerfully. "I don't think so. I must do my duty, or you would never care for me."

Ada had turned rather pale, and so, Mr. Jarndyce had her sit and sat beside her. "It's nothing but a friendly difference, my dear," he said. "We must tell you what it is, you being the theme. Are you afraid of what's coming?"

"Not if it comes from you, Cousin John," Ada replied, with a smile.

"Ada, my dear, you should know that Rick has chosen his profession for the last time," Mr. Jarndyce stated. "He has exhausted all his resources and is now bound for Ireland."

"It is true that my present resources are exhausted, and I am happy to know it," Richard said. "But what I have of certainty, sir, is not all I have."

"RICK!" my guardian exclaimed in a terrified manner, and in a changed voice. "For the love of God, do not form an expectation on the family curse! Do not ignore the horrible phantom that has haunted us for so many years. It is better to borrow, beg, better to die!"

We were all startled, but Mr. Jarndyce recovered quickly and became cheerful again. "My dear Ada, I agree these are strong words of advice. But I have seen a sight here in Bleak House. Hence, I recommend to both you and Richard that he depart from us agreeing that there is no contract between the two of you. This is for the sake of both Rick and you."

"It is better to state that you renounce all confidence in me and ask Ada to do the same," Richard replied. "I had hoped you would make the beginning that would keep you both happy," Mr. Jarndyce stated. "But there is time

for that yet. Make a new beginning. Both of you are still very young. You two are cousins still and nothing more." "You are harder than I'd have supposed you would be, sir," Richard exclaimed. "My dear boy, I'm harder with myself when I cause you pain. Ada, it is better for him that he should remain free and there be no youthful engagement between you two. Rick, it is better for her this way. You owe it to her. Do what is best for the other, and not for your own self."

Mr. Jarndyce urged Richard and Ada to begin afresh, as the time had not arrived for them to be pledged to each other. Then, Ada spoke. "Cousin Richard," she said, looking at him lovingly with her blue eyes. "After what Cousin John has said, there is no choice between us. You should not worry about me as you will leave me under his care. I can never doubt that you are very fond of me," Ada said, a little confused now. "I don't think you will fall in love with anyone else. But I'd like you to consider about that carefully too, as I'd like to see you happy. I

am very sorry to part from you, although I know it's for your own welfare. I shall always think of you with great affection and perhaps you will think of me a little, Cousin Richard," Ada said, and held out her trembling hand to Richard. "We are only cousins again, Richard, for the time being maybe. I pray a blessing for my cousin, wherever he goes!"

I found it strange that Richard was unable to forgive my guardian. But Richard was never as free and open with Mr. Jarndyce after that day. A wall of estrangement had started rising between the two.

Chapter Nine

Mother Dear

A favourite spot of mine existed in the park-woods where a seat had been constructed to offer an excellent view. The wood had been cleared and opened to further better this point of sight. The bright sunny landscape beyond that greeted the eyes was so pleasing that I rested there once a day.

One day, as I rested, I saw a figure approach through the wood. Initially, I could not make out what figure it was, because of the shadows of the branches on the ground. Slowly, it revealed itself to be a woman. It was Lady Dedlock! She approached me alone, and quickly. I was rendered motionless as she advanced with outstretched hands. Her face lacked her characteristic haughtiness. It

was a face I had longed and pined for ever since I was a child. I was both scared and faint.

"Miss Summerson, I fear I have startled you," she said, slowing down her pace. She offered me her hand, and its coldness fascinated me further. She sat down beside me, and my heart beat so violently now that it seemed I was about to die. She clasped me to her breast, kissed me, and wept. Then she fell down on her knees and cried, "Oh, my child! I am your wicked, unhappy mother! Oh, please try and forgive me!"

When I saw her suffering at my feet, I felt a deep gratitude towards the almighty. I was so altered that I could never disgrace her by any trace of likeness. No one could guess by looking at us that a tie existed between us. I lifted my mother up, begging her not to stoop before me in such pain and humiliation. I told her that I had forgiven her many years ago. My heart flowed with love for her; love that was natural which nothing in the past had or could alter. My duty was to bless and receive my mother, I said and held her in a loving embrace. She did the same, although our troubled minds were not entirely in peace.

"It is way too late to bless and receive me," my mother exclaimed. "I am fated to travel my dark road alone and it will lead me where it will. There are times when I fail to see my path before my guilty feet. I have brought upon this earthly punishment upon myself. I bear it and I hide it. This secret must be kept, as I have a husband, wretched and dishonoring creature that I am."

My mother wailed mournfully and covered her face in her hands. She shrunk in my embrace as if she was unwilling to be touched by me. I could not persuade her to rise despite my requests and endearments. She stated that she could only speak to me this way, as she had to appear haughty and disdainful elsewhere. She disclosed that she was well aware that I was alive. I was born to her before her marriage, and to save the family from the disgrace of a love child, her sister hid the baby, declaring it dead.

My mother gave me a letter for my eyes only. I was supposed to read it and destroy it and then consider her as dead. If I could believe that she loved me, despite this request, she asked me to do that.

"Does Mr. Jarndyce suspect?" she enquired suddenly.

"No, be assured that he does not," I replied, telling her what he had told me about my history. "He's a good, kind and rational man. If he knew…"

"Confide fully in him," my mother said. "You have my consent. A small gift from such a mother to her injured child. But do not tell me about it as there is still some pride left in me."

I requested mother to seek the help of Mr. Jarndyce, as he might be able to counsel her. But she refused, saying it was an impossible task. She must cross the desert that lay before her, alone.

"My dear child!" she pleaded. "Your kisses for the last time! Your arms upon my neck for the last time. We shall not meet again! Such is my reward and my doom! If you hear of Lady Dedlock, think of your mother beneath that mask! Think that the reality lies in her suffering, in her useless remorse, in her killing within her breast the love of her life. Forgive her if you can and then pray to the heavens to forgive her which it never will."

My mother left after one last kiss. I was alone, and calm. I went home slowly and read the letter. I learnt that I hadn't been abandoned by my mother.

Her elder sister had taken me away and reared me in complete secrecy. She ensured that my mother and I never met again. So, strangely, I had never borne a name. My mother had been startled when she first spotted me at church. She had thought how her little girl would look if she had been alive! She had concluded that she would have looked like me when she first saw me.

Chapter Ten

Jarndyce and Jarndyce

As the secret I had to keep was not mine, I did not confide in Ada. I felt I did not possess the right to share it even with my guardian, unless there was a great emergency. It was a weight to bear the burden of this secret alone, but I was determined to do so. So, when Ada was asleep, I was awake and the memory of my suffering mother made the night sorrowful.

Richard arrived in the evening to see us and greeted me with great brotherly warmth and love. I told him I was very happy to see him. "I have the greatest wish to talk to you, dear Esther," he stated. "I want you to understand me."

"I want you to understand someone else, Richard," I said, shaking my head.

"I suppose you mean John Jarndyce?" he asked.

"Yes."

"I am glad, as I am anxious to be understood on that subject," he said. "By you, mind you my dear. I am not accountable to Mr. Jarndyce or Mr. Anybody."

I was hurt that Richard took this tone. I asked him how he liked his profession and he typically said it was all right. "I don't know if I'll still like it when I am settled. Leave that botheration now. I am in town on leave."

"Really?"

"Yes, my Chancery interests need looking after before the long vacation," Richard stated, with a careless laugh, as I shook my head.

"It's not a pleasant subject," Richard said, observing my reaction.

I took him to Ada, and it was an awkward meeting. It wasn't difficult to read Ada's startled, blushing face. She loved him dearly and all three of us knew it. Meeting as cousins only was difficult!

I felt wicked, but I was unsure if Richard loved Ada as dearly. I dare say that he would have renewed their youthful romance but for the fact that he knew that Ada would never break the promise that she had made to her guardian. I was tormented with the thought that his influence existed here as well. Richard was postponing all things that needed his immediate attention till the Jarndyce and Jarndyce issue was settled.

Richard informed Ada in his most clever way, that he had not arrived to make any secret inroads on the terms she had accepted from her guardian. He had come openly to see both me and her and justify himself for the present terms on which he stood with Mr. Jarndyce. He requested my company for a conversation next morning, and I proposed to walk with him in the park at seven o'clock.

Richard was a little late the next morning, and it was a beautiful morning when we took our walk together. "This is a lovely place," Richard declared. "When I get affairs settled, I shall come down here and rest."

"Why not rest now?" I asked.

"That's not easy, Esther. If you were living in a house, with the constant threat of the roof being pulled down, you would find it hard to settle or rest. Just like me. There's no NOW for us suitors."

"Dear Richard, this is a bad beginning to our conversation."

"I knew you would say so, Esther."

"Not I alone, dear Richard. It was not I who warned you never to find a hope or expectation on the family curse."

"There you return to John Jarndyce," Richard exclaimed impatiently. "Well, he must be approached sooner or later, as he is the staple for what I have to say. How can you be so blind, dear Esther? Can't you see that he is an interested party? It would serve his interests that I know nothing about the suit, and care nothing about it. But that might not serve well for me!"

"Oh, Richard!" I exclaimed. "After living under his roof, and knowing him, how can you assume a thing like that?"

Richard reddened deeply, as he felt a pang of reproach at his accusation. He was silent for a while, and then stated, "Esther, I am sure you are aware that I am not a mean fellow. Suspicion and distrust are the poor qualities I possess, and this business is a bad one."

"Such misconstructions are alien to your nature, dear Richard."

"Come, sister come," Richard attempted a bit gaily. "Be fair with me. Both he and I have the misfortune of being under that influence. If it has twisted me a bit, it has twisted him a bit too. I'm not saying he isn't an honourable man, mind you. I'm sure he is. But this business taints everybody. You've heard him say so, many a time. How can HE escape?"

"That is because he is an uncommon man, Richard. A man who has been resolute enough to stay out of the circle."

"I am not sure about that, dear Esther," Richard stated. "It might be wise to project that outward indifference as it causes other parties to be lax about their own interests. Many things happen smoothly and conveniently then."

I could not reproach Richard any further as I only felt pity for him.

"I haven't come here to accuse John Jarndyce, Esther," Richard said. "I have come only to justify myself. We got along very well when I was a boy. But the moment I displayed an interest in the suit, I was asked to break

off with Ada rather unfairly by John Jarndyce. He has no right to declare if I am fit or not for Ada. I must maintain my rights and Ada's whether it pleases or displeases him. After a lot of thought, this is the conclusion I have arrived at. I have written to him about it that we should be open about the issue rather than covert. I thank him for everything he has done for me, and we go separate ways. Under one of the wills in dispute, I should take much more than him. I'm not stating that this will be established, but there is a chance. I know my views might appear harsh to both you and Ada, but if you only applied yourself to the papers like I did at Kenge's, you would find me justified."

"But is there truth and justice among these papers, Richard?"

"There is truth and justice somewhere in the case, Esther."

"Or was once, a long time ago," I replied.

"It is and must be brought out," Richard insisted. "To make Ada receive a bribe and hush-money is not the way. You say the suit is changing me, but doesn't John Jarndyce say that the suit has changed anyone having a share in

it? I have the greater right on my side when I say I shall strive all I can to bring it to a close."

"All you can, Richard? Do you think others haven't tried in all these years? Has the situation been eased after so many failures?"

"It can't go on forever," Richard stated fiercely. "I am young and earnest. Energy and determination have often worked wonders. While others have just half thrown themselves into it, I have devoted myself to it. It is the object of my life."

"Oh, dear Richard, so much the worse," I exclaimed.

"Don't be afraid for me, dear Esther. You are a good, fine girl; but you have your prepossessions. This business makes natural relations incompatible. It is quite possible that I find that I am mistaken about John Jarndyce when all this is over. My head might clear once I am free of this, and I might agree to whatever you say today. I want Ada to understand that I have purpose and reason to judge John Jarndyce, and I am not fickle or presumptuous. I wish to approach her through you, as she has great respect and regard for her cousin John. I know you shall soften

the approach I take, even though you disapprove of it."

"Is that all you want me to tell Ada?" I asked.

"Tell her also that John Jarndyce replied to my letter, and tried to argue me out of my views, stating that they would make no difference to him or the case. Let Ada know that I am looking after her interests as well as mine, as we are both in the same boat. Tell her not to believe any rumours about me. I am not accountable to John Jarndyce anymore, as I am of age, but I shall not ask Ada to renew our engagement as she is still a ward of the court. I shall wait till she is free to act for herself. If you tell Ada this in your kind and considerate way, Esther, you will do a great service to me. I shall then knock Jarndyce and Jarndyce on the head with greater energy."

"You place great confidence in me, Richard, and yet, you will not take my advice."

"Impossible on this matter, dear Esther. Any other subject, readily."

As if there was another subject in his life!

"Are you in debt again, Richard?"

"Of course I am," he replied. "Such an object cannot be

achieved without expenses. You forget or are unaware that under either will, Ada and I take something. To spend a small sum to gain a larger one is only sensible."

I sensed the danger Richard was approaching and tried to warn him. Although he listened patiently, none of my words had any effect on him. I decided to try Ada's influence and told her everything Richard had told me. It made her very unhappy and Ada told me that it did not matter if Richard was ruined or prosperous after the suit, her heart would still be full of love for him. Just as he thought of her in all his erroneous ways, she would think of him at all times. She would not think of her delights if she could not attend to his.

Did she keep her word?

Chapter Eleven

The Secret

How does it matter how much I thought of my living mother who wanted me to think of her as dead? I could not think of approaching her or establishing communication by writing to her. I only thought of the peril I might add to her already perilous life. I was aware that my very existence was a danger to her, and was terrorized ever since I knew the secret. I could not utter her name or hear it being spoken. I shut my ears if conversation referred to her. I mentally counted, repeated something, or simply exited the room. I did all this for fear that my actions might betray her. It does not matter how I recalled my mother's voice, and how I longed to hear it again! I wondered how this strange feeling was so new to me. I passed and

repassed my mother's house in town, afraid to look at it. I might as well leave that behind me and move forward.

Ada and I spoke about Richard with our guardian many times. Ada was grief struck that her kind cousin could do so much wrong. But she couldn't blame Richard, being faithful to him. "Rick is mistaken, my dear," my guardian would say to Ada kindly. "We are all mistaken over and over again. Time will set him right." Our guardian had tried everything with Richard to open his eyes. He had written to him, met and spoke with him, and tried all gentle and persuasive methods. But Richard had been deaf and blind to everything. Jarndyce and Jarndyce had possessed him like the devil and he wanted to see the end of the suit. "It is better to leave the poor fellow alone, than to remonstrate with him, my guardian stated to me.

I had decided that I would confide in my guardian about my terrible secret, as it was so painful that I needed his help. I sought him among his books after Ada and I had retired for the night. "May I come in, guardian?" I asked. "Surely, little woman. What is the matter?"

"I wished to say a word about myself," I stated, as he shut his book and put a chair for me. "What concerns you, concerns me Esther," he said. "I am as ready to hear as you are to speak."

"I have much need of your advice and support, dear guardian," I stated, as he looked a bit alarmed.

"Guardian, do you remember Lady Dedlock speak to you about her sister?"

"Of course I do."

"Do you remember that she and her sister had differed to go separate ways?"

"Yes."

"That sister is my first remembrance."

"No!" he cried. "Yes, guardian! HER sister is my mother!" I exclaimed.

He spoke tenderly and wisely to me and put everything so plainly before me that I felt deep gratitude towards him. I never loved him more dearly, and never thanked him as much as I did that night. He took me to my room and kissed me at the door. When I lay down to sleep, all that went through my mind was how to be busy, good, and devoted enough to my guardian, to show him how much I loved and honoured him.

Chapter Twelve

The Letter and the Reply

My guardian summoned me to his room the next morning, and I told him what I had left untold the night before. He said that there was nothing to be done but keep the secret and avoid another such encounter. I thanked him wholeheartedly. He asked me to stay for a moment when I was about to leave. "My dear Esther, I have wanted to tell you something for a very long time," he declared. "I have had some difficulty in approaching it and I still do. But I wish to say it. Would you object if I wrote it?"

"Dear guardian, how could I object to your writing anything for ME to read?"

"Can you fully trust me and rely on what I have to say to you, Esther?" he asked, looking into my eyes.

"Thoroughly," I replied.

"Give me your hand, dear girl," he said. He held my hand, holding me lightly with his arm and stared into my face in that same protecting manner that had made his house my home instantly.

"You have brought about changes in me, little woman, ever since the winter day in the stage-coach. You have done me a lot of good since then."

"Ah, guardian, what a lot of good you have done for me since then!"

"That is not to be remembered now," he stated.

"That can never be forgotten," I replied.

"It is best if that is forgotten for a while, Esther. Just remember that nothing can change me as you now know me. Are you quite assured of that, my dear?"

"Yes," I replied.

"That's a lot. In fact, that's everything. But if you have the slightest doubt regarding that, I shall refrain from writing the letter."

"I am certain, guardian."

He said nothing about this for a week, after which I received his letter. It was so full of love for me and the selfless caution it contained overwhelmed me. It displayed so much care for me that I was blinded to read it all at once. I had to read it thrice before I put it down. I had guessed about the contents earlier, but now I was certain. My guardian's letter asked me if I would be the mistress of Bleak House.

It was not a love letter, even though much love was expressed. The letter was written just as he would speak to me at any point in time. As I read his letter, I heard his voice and even saw his face. I was under the influence of his kind, protective manner in each line he had written. He wrote as if all the good deeds had been mine and the dormant feelings they had awakened in him. He wrote about me being young, while he was past the prime of youth; on his reaching a ripe age, while I was still a child. The letter stated that I would gain nothing by such a marriage and lose nothing by rejecting it, for no new relation could increase the affection that he had

towards me. He was convinced that whatever decision I would make would be right. I was always supposed to remember that I owed him nothing and that he was my debtor instead. He had thought about our future often, foreseeing that the time might arrive when Ada would leave us when she was of age. Our regular mode of life would be disrupted then and this thought had made him reflect on the proposal that he had finally made. If I felt that I wanted to become the companion of his remaining life, I was to consider this proposal with ample time at my disposal. His old relation would still hold good even if I refused his proposal, and he would still take care of me. He knew that his affection for me would remain unchanged, regardless of my decision.

I felt, and I knew, that there was only one course of action left for me; to devote my life to his happiness, even though that was to thank him poorly for all his goodness. Yet, I cried a lot. I cried as the prospect was strange, and I cried because I was very happy, thankful and hopeful. Then I thought about a situation when my guardian had married

someone else. How would I have felt then? That change would have been so strange indeed! That mere thought presented my life in a bleak and blank form!

The next morning, I entered the breakfast-room to discover my guardian in his usual frank, free and open manner. There was no constraint in his manner, nor in mine. He did not utter a word about the letter, as I thought or hoped he would. A week passed by in the expectation that my guardian would speak to me about the letter. But he never did. I grew uneasy as I thought that I should reply to his letter. But I could not write anything that seemed to be a good reply. Each night, I thought I'd wait one more day. A week flew by, but he still did not speak a word.

One afternoon, the three of us were going out riding. I got dressed before Ada and came downstairs, to see my guardian staring out the drawing-room window, his back towards me.

"It's you little woman, is it?" he turned smilingly, as I entered, and looked out again.

I had resolved to speak to him now. In fact, I had come down purposefully.

"Guardian," I stated, trembling and hesitating, "When would you like to receive a reply to the letter?"

"When it's ready, my dear," he replied.

"I think it's ready now," I said, putting my arms around his neck and kissing him.

"Is this the mistress of Bleak House?" he asked.

"Yes!" I replied. We went out riding after that, but I said nothing to my precious Ada about it.

Chapter Thirteen

Enlightenment

"We should go and see Richard," I proposed to Ada one morning and was surprised to see her hesitate. She wasn't as enthusiastic as I had expected.

"My dear Ada," I enquired. "You haven't had any difference with Richard, have you?"

"No, Esther."

"You haven't heard of him, perhaps?"

"I have," Ada replied sadly. I could not fathom what had happened by seeing tears in her eyes and love in her face. I asked her if I should go to Richard's place all by myself. Ada said no to that and consented to accompany me.

It was one of those dreary days with drops of chilly rain falling periodically. The colourless day made

everything seem harsh; the houses we passed, frowned at us, the dust threatened to swallow us and the smoke swooped at us. We had to locate Symond's Inn and Ada said it was near Chancery Lane. We found it soon enough. We had to find out the number after that, and Ada suggested that it was perhaps in the corner there. It actually was!

I had wanted to knock, but Ada suggested we turn the handle and walk in. As we did so, we came upon Richard, poring over a table full of dusty bundles of papers. They seemed to me dusty mirrors that reflected his own mind. Jarndyce and Jarndyce! The ominous words were everywhere.

"You would have found Woodcourt if you had come a little earlier," Richard revealed, after receiving us affectionately. "The good fellow finds time to look in when he can, when people having half his work would think of not coming. He brightens up this place with his cheerfulness and it darkens when he leaves. He's not as sanguine as me, Ada. But he does not know the mysteries,

being an outsider. We have gone into the labyrinth, while he hasn't."

I saw how large and sunken his eyes were. His lips were dry and his finger-nails bitten away. I suggested that a change from this unhealthy place might do Richard good and he laughed.

"It might do me good in one of two ways. Either the suit must end or the suitor. But it shall be the suit, my dear girl!"

The last words were addressed to Ada and this commentary seemed distressing to me. His hopefulness had always pained me more than his despondency, and I thought that self-reproach, premature anxiety, and disappointment would accompany him to his deathbed.

"But this work makes me so tired sometimes," Richard confessed, as he walked across the room and sunk upon the sofa.

Suddenly, Ada cast away her bonnet, kneeling beside Richard, so that her golden hair cascaded like sunlight over his head. She clasped two arms around his

neck, and turned towards me. Such a loving and devoted face it was!

"Dear Esther," she declared quietly, "I am not going home again!"

All at once, realization dawned on me.

"I shall stay with my dear husband. We have been married for more than two months. Go home without me Esther, as I shall never go home anymore."

With those words, Ada held Richard's head to her breast. If ever I saw a love that only death could alter, it was then before my eyes!

Richard urged Ada to tell me everything. Before she could come to me, I went and took Ada in my arms.

"My pet! My love! My poor, poor girl!" I said. I pitied Ada so much but was also fond of Richard. Yet, I could not help but pity her.

"Forgive me Esther!" she said. "Will cousin John forgive me?"

"To doubt that even for a moment, my dear, is to do him a great wrong," I replied. As to me, what had I to forgive!

I dried Ada's eyes and sat beside her and Richard on the sofa. They told me how they had gotten married one morning. Although I pitied them both, I also felt a kind of pride in their love. I had never experienced such pain and pleasure simultaneously, and I was unsure which emotion dominated over the other. Ada pulled out her wedding-ring from her bosom, kissed it and wore it. I recalled how Ada had put her hand beneath her pillow at night when she wore the ring so I couldn't see it. It was finally time for me to return and Ada broke down completely. She clung around my neck, calling me dear names, and lamenting what she would do without me! I held her tightly, and Ada smiled at me through her tears. I kissed Ada one last time, laughed, and ran away.

Oh, how I wept when I reached downstairs! It seemed I had lost Ada forever! I was so lost and lonely without her! I took a coach home after I had recovered. I discovered that my guardian was not at home. He did not return for dinner and I cried some more. I was not used to being without my darling Ada. My mind dwelt on the

unhappy setting where I had left her. I longed to be close to her and protect her. This feeling was so overpowering that I decided to return in the evening and look up at her windows. This notion was foolish, but did not seem so to me back then, and does not even now.

I left at dusk and it was dark when I arrived at their strange lodging. I spotted a light behind the yellow blinds, and walked past curiously thrice or four times, staring up. Then, I stole upstairs quietly and listened in silence for a few minutes. I thought I heard the murmur of their young voices. I kissed the door and came downstairs and this visit really did me good. I felt as if it had brought me close to Ada for a moment.

I returned home feeling much better. I discovered my guardian standing thoughtfully by the window. "Little woman, you have been crying," he exclaimed, as he saw me. "Yes, guardian, I'm afraid I have been, a little," I replied. "Ada has been in such distress and she is so very sorry, guardian."

"Is she married, my dear?" he enquired. I told him

everything and how Ada had begged for his forgiveness. "She has no need of it," he declared. "God bless her and her husband!"

But his first impulse was pity, just like mine. "Poor girl!" he exclaimed. "Poor Ada! Poor Rick!"

We were quiet after that, and he broke the silence with a sigh. "Well, my dear," he stated sorrowfully. "Bleak House is thinning fast!"

"But its mistress remains, guardian," I declared timidly. "She will do all that she can to make it happy!"

Chapter Fourteen

Perspective

I fell ill during one of our London visits. Mr. Woodcourt's mother had come to stay with us here on my guardian's invitation. When I was better, my guardian expressed his wish to stay on in London for six months or more.

"Leave Bleak House in the meanwhile?" I asked.

"Yes, my dear. Bleak House must learn how to take care of itself. It's a long way from Ada, who needs you."

"It's so much like you, guardian, to think of a happy surprise for both of us."

"You may extol me for that virtue, my dear. But the truth is that I want to hear as much about Ada as you do, and as often. Also of Rick, poor fellow!"

"Have you seen Mr. Woodcourt this morning, guardian?"

"I see him every morning, Dame Durden."

"Does he say the same of Richard?"

"The same. He is unaware of any direct bodily illness that Rick has. In fact, he thinks he has none. Yet, he is not easy about him."

"Poor Richard! When will he wake up from his delusion?"

"He will not do so now, my dear," my guardian replied. "The more he suffers, the more he will be against me, as he considers me to be the main representative of his suffering."

"How unreasonable!" I exclaimed.

"Ah, Dame Trot!" my guardian said. "There is nothing reasonable about Jarndyce and Jarndyce! There is lack of reason and justice at the top, and at the bottom. Unreason and injustice have co-existed from beginning to end, if it ever has an end that is. How does one expect poor Rick, always hovering around it, to grab reason out of it? I have begged Woodcourt in particular and now I beg of you, my dear. Do not raise this subject with Rick! Let it rest as sometime, perhaps next week, next month, or even next year, he will see me with clearer vision. I am willing to wait!"

"You mentioned, dear guardian, that Mr. Woodcourt would give a long trial to another country. Have you been advising him in this regard?" I enquired.

"Yes, pretty often, dear."

"Has he decided to do so?"

"I think not."

"Some other prospect has presented itself to him, perhaps?"

"Yes, perhaps," my guardian replied. "There is an opening for a medical attendant for the poor at a place in Yorkshire for almost six months later. It is a bustling place, with a pleasant location. The opening is suitable for a man whose hopes and ambition are above the ordinary, but to whom good service and a way of usefulness is also important. I suppose all generous spirits are ambitious, but the ambition that walks calmly upon such a path, instead of trying to fly over it repeatedly, is the kind I care for. It is for a man like Woodcourt."

"Will he get this appointment?"

"Why, I cannot be confident about that," my guardian stated smilingly. "But he has a high reputation, and I do believe that the best man has the best chance. To you, it

might not appear to be a fine endowment as it is a very commonplace affair, my dear. It is an appointment that requires a lot of work and fetches a small amount of pay. But better things will materialise out of it, it may be hoped."

"The poor of the place have every reason to rejoice if Mr. Woodcourt gets the job, guardian."

"You are right, little woman. I am sure they will."

I began visiting Ada every day. Usually, I went in the mornings, but whenever I had an hour to spare, I rushed off to Chancery Lane. Both Ada and Richard were happy to see me and their faces brightened up when I arrived. I never knocked. I just opened the door and entered. Richard was mostly absent when I came. He would be seated at his table when he was around, covered with papers that were never disturbed. Sometimes, I would spot him lounging about in the neighbourhood, biting his nails.

Richard had gone for a walk with Mr. Woodcourt when I arrived one day.

"Esther, my dearest," Ada said to me. "Richard is always unwell, and I'm most easy when he is with Mr. Allan Woodcourt. We have to thank you for that."

I corrected Ada, saying that Mr. Woodcourt had arrived at her Cousin John's house, and had known us all there. That was how Richard and Mr. Woodcourt had struck up a fine friendship. But Ada insisted on giving me the credit, and I let her have her way.

"I want to be a very good wife, Esther," Ada said, trembling. "You shall teach me."

I was stunned.

"When I married Richard, I knew very well what was before him. I was perfectly happy with you, Esther, and had never known anxiety or trouble. I was so loved and cared for, but I perceived the danger Richard was in."

"I know, my darling," I replied.

"I nursed a little hope after marrying him that I might be able to make him see his mistake. He might see it in new light as my husband and not pursue the matter so desperately for my sake! But he still does. Esther, if I didn't have that hope, I would have still married him. Just the same! Do not think, dearest Esther that I fail to see what you do, and I do not fear what you fear. The greatest wisdom in the world could barely know Richard better than my love!"

Ada's speech was soft and modest and her trembling hand seemed to agitatedly move to and fro upon the silent notes. Oh, my dear, dear girl!

"I see him at his worst each day," Ada continued, "I watch him in his sleep and am aware of every change of his face. I was quite determined when I married him, and if heaven would help me, it would never display my unhappiness to him to make him unhappier than he already is. I never want him to see me troubled when he comes home. I want him to see what he loved in me, every time he looks at me. This supports me and I married him to do this."

I sensed her trembling again and waited for what was to come. I had a strange feeling I knew what it would be!

"I look forward a little while," Ada stated after a pause. "I don't know what great aid I might receive. But when Richard sees the little creature lying on my breast, it is possible that he or she is more eloquent than I have ever been. The creature might have greater power to win Richard back," Ada said, as we held each other.

"If that little creature fails as well, Esther," she said. "I shall still look forward, thinking that when I am old,

or even dead, maybe a beautiful daughter will be proud of him and a blessing to him. Or perhaps, a brave, generous and handsome man may walk in the sun with him saying, 'I thank God this is my father! Ruined by a fatal inheritance and restored through me!"

What a heart that sweet girl possessed which beat so fast against mine!

"These hopes make me stronger, dear Esther, and I know they will," Ada declared. "But sometimes, they disappear before a dread that arises when I look at Richard."

I tried to cheer her up and asked what it was she feared. Sobbing violently, Ada revealed, "He might not live to see his child!"

Chapter Fifteen

A Discovery

The months glided away. Ada was the same old star in a miserable corner and Richard had been reduced to a more haggard and miserable state. He haunted the courts day after day. He sat there listlessly the whole day long, even when he knew that there wasn't the slightest chance of the suit being mentioned. Richard became one of the stock signs of the place and even his cheerful disposition had almost abandoned him. I say almost because Richard displayed signs of cheerfulness only in the presence of Mr. Woodcourt. Only Mr. Woodcourt could divert Richard's attention for a couple of hours at a time and rouse him from a state of lethargy of mind and body that alarmed us all. Ada was correct that Richard chased his errors even more desperately for her. The desire to retrieve what

he had lost was intensified further for his young wife's sake. This grief was transformed into the madness of a gamester.

I was there at all hours now. I returned home in a coach when I visited at night and sometimes my guardian would meet me in the neighbourhood, to walk me home. One evening, he had asked me to meet him at eight o' clock, but I was unable to leave. I was working for Ada and had a few stitches to be finished. Mr. Woodstock accompanied me when I left, as it was dusk already.

But my guardian was absent when I arrived at our usual meeting place. We waited for half an hour, but there was no sign of him. Then, Mr. Woodcourt proposed to walk me home. This was the first walk we had taken together, besides the short one occasionally to the usual meeting place. Arriving home, we discovered that both my guardian and Mrs. Woodcourt were out.

We stood by the open window overlooking the street when Mr. Woodcourt spoke to me. I learned that he loved me dearly! Oh, it was too late to know it now! Far too late! That was the first ungrateful thought that rushed through my head. "I have always feared that I should profess my love for you in vain," Mr. Woodcourt broke the silence.

"I have fulfilled both my hopes and fears tonight. I think I have said enough as I distress you."

I wept as I was sorrowful for the loss he had sustained.

"Dear Mr. Woodcourt," I said. "Before we part tonight, I have something to say. I shall never be able to say it exactly as I wish. But I am grateful for your generosity, and shall treasure its memory till my dying hour. As you are unaware of my history, I know your love is noble and faithful. What you have said couldn't have affected me if it was uttered by someone else. But it shall not be lost, and will only make me better."

Covering his eyes with his hand, Mr. Woodcourt turned away from me. Alas! I was unworthy of those tears! "I hope to have the pleasure of your company in tending Ada and Richard and, hopefully, in many happier scenes of life as well," I stated. "But I shall never forget this night, Mr. Woodcourt, as long as my heart beats. I can never forget the pride and joy of being loved by you."

He took my hand and kissed it. I was encouraged as he was himself again.

"I hope you have succeeded in your professional endeavor," I said.

"I have, thanks to Mr. Jarndyce's help."

"Heaven bless him for it and heaven bless you in all that you do," I said. "What will happen to poor Richard when you are gone?"

"I am not required to leave yet," he replied. "I would not desert him, even if I had to leave."

"Before I say goodnight, Mr. Woodcourt," I said. "I must say that the future is clear and bright before me. I am both happy and fortunate, and neither desire nor regret anything."

He replied that he was glad to hear that.

"I have been the recipient of the untiring goodness of the best of human beings from my childhood," I stated. "I am bound to them by every tie of gratitude, attachment and love, and nothing I do in my entire life could express the feelings of a single day."

"I share those feelings," he replied. "You speak of Mr. Jarndyce."

"You are well aware of his virtues," I said. "But few are aware of the greatness of his character, like me. His best qualities have been revealed in order to shape a future that makes me so happy."

We said goodnight, and as he left, I stood at the dark window, watching the street. His love had announced itself so suddenly that only a minute after he had left me, my vision was obscured by my tears. But these were not tears of sorrow or regret. He had called me the beloved of his life and he had stated that I would be dear to him regardless of the future. No, it was not too late to hear those words from his lips, for it was not too late to be animated by them to be good, contented, true and grateful. How easy my path was, so much easier than his!

Chapter Sixteen

An Upcoming Marriage

I did not have the courage to see anyone that night, not even myself. I was afraid my tears might reproach me and went up to my room. I prayed in the dark, and lay down to sleep. I did not need any light to read my guardian's letter, as I knew the contents by heart. I took the letter, repeated its contents by its own clear light of love and integrity and slept with the letter on my pillow.

I woke up very early in the morning. "Why, little woman, you look fresher than your flowers," my guardian exclaimed, when he saw me. It only made me feel worse! After breakfast, I decided to see my guardian in his room. He was writing a letter.

"Well, Dame Durden," he said. "You want money?"

"No, I have plenty at hand."

"There was never another like Dame Durden, to make money last," he said.

"Have I been remiss in something, dear guardian?" I asked.

"You have been everything I could desire, my love," he replied.

"I am glad to hear that, indeed. Dear guardian, perhaps you expect me to renew the subject. Let me tell you that I shall be the mistress of Bleak House whenever it pleases you."

"I am sorry that I have been totally preoccupied with the thought of poor Rick," he stated. "Little woman, when shall we give Bleak House its mistress?"

"When you please, guardian."

"Next month?"

"Next month, dear guardian."

"The day I shall take the happiest and best step of my life," he stated happily. "The day I shall be a man happier, and more enviable than any other man in the world. The day I shall present Bleak House its little mistress. It shall be next month then."

I placed my arms around his neck and kissed him just like the day when I had brought him my answer to his letter.

Chapter Seventeen

Another Discovery

My guardian gave me a sealed paper one morning. "This is for next month, my dear," he said. I discovered two hundred pounds in it and began to make the necessary arrangements quietly. I made the purchases according to my guardian's taste which were now very familiar to me. I arranged my wardrobe in an attempt to please him. I was convinced that we would be married in a simple and private ceremony, considering all the circumstances. I only wished to invite Ada to my wedding.

The only exception I made was for Mrs. Woodcourt. I informed her that I was going to get married to my guardian and that we had been engaged for some time. She highly approved of this alliance. The time was very

near when my guardian was summoned to Yorkshire on Mr. Woodcourt's business. A letter from him informed me about it as I returned home from Ada's one night. He asked me to join him in the country the next morning, and informed me that my place was taken in the stagecoach, and the time it would leave.

A journey was least expected by me then, but I packed whatever was necessary in half an hour and left early the next morning. As I travelled all day, I wondered why he had summoned me there. I found my guardian waiting for me at the end of the journey. Supper was ready at the hotel and when we were alone at the table, he addressed me, "You must be full of curiosity, undoubtedly, little woman, to learn why I brought you here?"

"Well, guardian, I must admit that I am curious about it."

"My dear, I have always wished to convey my gratitude to Woodcourt for his inestimable services to my young cousins and his value to all of us. When it was decided that Woodcourt should settle here, an idea came to my head that I request him to accept a suitable little place to reside in. Therefore, I arranged for such a place to be looked out for and it was found on rather easy terms. I

have been in the process of touching it up for him, and making it worthy to live in. Unfortunately, I do not possess the genuine qualities of a housekeeper to discern if things are the way they ought to be. So, I thought it prudent to send for the best little housekeeper known to me, to seek her opinion and advice. And here she is, laughing and crying both together!" my guardian stated, with a smile.

I could not articulate a word to tell him because he was so good and admirable. Dismissing my thanks, he asked me why I sobbed.

"It is with exquisite pleasure and a thankful heart, guardian," I replied.

"I am delighted that you approve of my plan, just as I thought you would. I meant it as a pleasant surprise for the little mistress of Bleak House."

I cried with pleasure when I went to bed that night.

It was a beautiful summer morning the next day, and after breakfast, we reached to see the house, arm in arm. He opened a gate in a side wall and we entered a flower garden where the beds and flowers were laid out just like the way mine were at home. We crossed a pretty little orchard with cherries and apple-trees, to reach the

BLEAK HOUSE

house. It was a small, rustic cottage of doll's rooms; but a lovely place, tranquil and lovely!

"Last but not the least," my guardian declared, "The name of this house."

"What is it, guardian?" I asked. He led me to the porch, and written over it was, Bleak House.

Leading me to a seat and sitting down beside me, my guardian took my hand in his. "My darling girl, whatever there has been between us, I hope, has made you happy," he said. "When I wrote you that letter, I had my own happiness in mind; but I had yours too. I don't need to ask myself if I might ever have ever renewed my long cherished dream of making you my wife one day, had the circumstances been different. But I did renew that dream. I wrote you the letter and you replied. Are you following me, my child?"

I was cold and shaking violently. But I was listening attentively.

"It does not matter when I began to doubt if what I had done would make you happy. I had no doubt at all when Woodcourt came home."

I held him around the neck and wept on his breast.

"I am your guardian and your father now," he said gently. "Rest confidently here!"

He was as soothing as the rustling of the leaves and spoke as clearly as the sunshine. "I had no doubt that you would be happy and contented with me, dear girl. But I also saw that you would be happier with Allan Woodcourt. I have long been in his confidence, although he was in mine only a few hours ago before you arrived here. I took Mrs. Woodcourt into confidence separately and informed her that her son loved my ward. I told her that I was sure that my ward loved her son as well, but was forced to sacrifice her love because of a sense of duty and affection. I told her the entire story and Allan Woodcourt spoke to you with my permission, my dear. He was to come and tell me whatever had transpired, which he did. On this day, I give Bleak House its little mistress! Before God, this is the brightest day in all my life!"

He raised me up and I realized that we were no longer alone. My husband – I have addressed him by that name for seven happy years now – stood by my side.

"Allan," my guardian stated. "Receive from me a willing gift, the best wife that man ever had. You deserve her

more than anyone else. Receive her with the little home she brings you. Do let me share its happiness sometimes. What do I sacrifice? Nothing at all!"

As he kissed me, I saw the tears in his eyes. "Esther dearest, there is a kind of parting in this too, after all these years. I'm aware that my mistake has caused you some distress. Forgive your old guardian and restore him to his old place in your heart. Take my dear, Allan."

He walked away from us, turning around to say, "No one should thank me anymore, as I return to my old bachelor habits. If one disregards this warning, I shall run away and never come back."

It was a day of great happiness and bliss! We were to be married before the end of the month, but when we decided to move into our new house, depended on Richard and Ada.

Chapter Eighteen

Beginning a New World

The term had commenced and Mr. Kenge intimated my guardian that the cause would come on in two days. I was hopeful that there would be a decision. Allan and I decided to go to the court that morning. The day's business had begun when we arrived and the crowd at the Chancery was full to the door. A gentleman informed us that the cause of Jarndyce and Jarndyce was over after we enquired. Over for the day? We asked. No, he said, over for good!

We were stunned. Could it be true that the will had set things right at last? Were Richard and Ada finally rich? It was too good to be true! The suspense was short-lived,

as people came streaming out. Mr. Kenge arrived to greet us and asked if Mr. Jarndyce was here. He said it was good when I told him that he was absent. Mr. Kenge informed us that the whole estate had been absorbed in the costs of the case.

"This will break Richard's heart!" Allan exclaimed. He rushed inside to see to Richard, while I went home. I told my guardian what had happened and he escorted me to Ada's house in the afternoon. He waited while I went upstairs. Ada hugged me and told me that Richard had asked to see me several times. Allan had discovered Richard sitting in a corner of the court like a statue. On being roused, he had attempted speaking strongly to the judge. He had been restrained by a mouth full of blood, and Allan had brought him home.

Richard was lying on a sofa, with his eyes closed when I entered. His face was devoid of colour and he looked totally worn out. I sat beside him silently, and he said weakly with a smile, "Dame Durden, kiss me my dear!"

It was both surprising and comforting to see Richard cheerful in his low state. He said he didn't have words

to express how happy my intended marriage with Allan made him. He stated he would be present at our wedding if he could stand upon his feet. It was not a good idea for Richard to talk so much and we were silent when he chose to be silent. Ada leaned upon his pillow, holding his head upon her arm.

Evening had set in when I spotted my guardian standing in the little hall. "Who is that Dame Durden?" Richard asked me. I glanced at Allan for advice, and he nodded yes. I bent over Richard and told him. My guardian had seen what had transpired and was beside me softly and instantly. He laid his hand on Richard's.

"Oh, sir," Richard exclaimed. "You are a good man, such a good man!"

Then, Richard burst into tears for the first time in my guardian's presence.

"My dear Rick," my guardian stated. "The clouds have all cleared away and it is bright now. We were all bewildered, but can see now. How are you, my dear boy?"

"I am very weak, sir," Richard replied. "I hope to be stronger. I have to begin the world."

"Truly! Well said!" my guardian exclaimed. "There is nothing more I want than to see Dame Durden and Woodcourt's house, sir," Richard requested. "If I am removed there, I think I shall recover better than anywhere else."

"Why, I have been thinking the same, Rick," my guardian stated.

"I say nothing of Ada. Look at her, sir! See her bending over my pillow when she is in need to rest upon one herself. Oh my dear love! My poor girl!" Richard exclaimed. He tried to raise himself, and Allan helped him so that Ada could hold him on her bosom, which was what he wanted. A smile illuminated his face as she bent to kiss him. He slowly laid his face down upon her bosom, held her round her neck, and with one parting sob, began the world. Not this world, oh no, not this one! He began the world that sets this one right!

I have been the mistress of Bleak House for seven happy years now. They gave my darling into my arms and I never left her alone. The little child who was expected to do so much was born before the turf was planted on

its father's grave. It was a boy who was given his father's name, Richard! Slowly, time healed Ada's wounds, and my darling walked in my country garden with her infant in her arms. I was married then and the happiest of the happy! My guardian asked Ada when she would come home. "Both houses are your home, my dear. But the older Bleak House claims priority," he said. "When you and my boy are strong enough, come and take possession of your home!"

He was her guardian again, as well as the boy's. He had an old association with that name after all. So she called him guardian and has called him guardian ever since. The children know him by the same name. I say the children because I have been blessed with two little daughters.

About the Author

■ Charles Dickens (1812–1870)

Charles John Huffam Dickens was an English writer. He created some of the world's best-known fictional characters and is widely regarded as the greatest novelist of the Victorian era. He has been termed a literary genius and his novels and short stories enjoy lasting popularity.

Dickens left school to work in a factory when his father was put in a debtors' prison. Despite lacking a formal education, Dickens edited a weekly journal for 20 years, wrote 15 novels, five novellas, hundreds of short stories and non-fiction articles. Over the course of his writing career, classics like *Oliver Twist, A Christmas Carol, Nicholas Nickleby, David Copperfield, A Tale of Two Cities* and *Great Expectations* were published.

Bleak House is a nineteenth century novel, first published as a serial between March 1852 and September 1853. The story is told partly by the novel's heroine, Esther Summerson and partly by an omniscient narrator. At the centre of *Bleak House* is a long-running legal case, Jarndyce and Jarndyce, and Dickens uses this case to satirize the English judicial system. This novel helped support a judicial reform movement, which culminated in the enactment of legal reform in the 1870s.

■ List of Main Characters

Esther Summerson: She is the narrator and the protagonist. Esther is an orphan who becomes the housekeeper at Bleak House when she, Ada, and Richard are taken in by Mr. Jarndyce. Everyone loves Esther, who is selfless and lovable. Although Esther eventually does find her mother, circumstances prevent them from developing a relationship. At first a hesitant, insecure narrator, Esther's confidence in her storytelling grows and she controls the narrative skillfully.

John Jarndyce: He is Esther's guardian and the master of Bleak House. Mr. Jarndyce becomes the guardian of the orphans Ada and Richard, and takes Esther in as a companion for Ada. Generous but uncomfortable with others' gratitude, Mr. Jarndyce provides a warm, happy home for the three young people. When Esther is an adult, he proposes marriage, but he eventually withdraws his offer when he realizes she's in love with Allan Woodcourt. Instead, he brings them both together.

Ada Clare: She is Jarndyce's ward. Kind, sweet, and naïve, Ada becomes Esther's closest confidante and greatest source of happiness. She falls in love with Richard, and although they eventually marry and have a baby, she never finds full happiness with him because of his obsession with the Jarndyce and Jarndyce lawsuit.

Richard Carstone: He is Jarndyce's ward. Affable but lazy, Richard can't decide on a career and seems to have no passion for a particular field. Eventually, he becomes obsessed with Jarndyce and Jarndyce and ultimately sacrifices his life for the lawsuit. He pursues the suit for Ada's sake but never succeeds in providing a real home for her.

■ Questions

Chapter 1

- *What did the term 'Jarndyce and Jarndyce' signify?*
- *Describe the two regulars who visited the court during this suit?*

Chapter 2

- *Who was Esther? How did she describe her godmother?*
- *What did Esther's godmother tell her about her mother?*

Chapter 3

- *What was the growlery? Describe in detail.*
- *What favour did Mr. Jarndyce ask of Esther?*

Chapter 4

- *Why was Richard unable to choose a profession for himself?*
- *What profession did Richard settle on finally?*

Chapter 5

- *Why was Richard so obsessive about the lawsuit?*
- *What did Mr. Jarndyce reveal to Esther about her past?*

Chapter 6

- *Who was Lady Dedlock? What effect did she have on Esther when she first saw her? Why?*
- *Where did Mr. Jarndyce, Ada and Esther take shelter from the storm? What happened after that?*

Chapter 7

- *Why was Richard in a miserable situation?*
- *What profession did Richard have his mind set on now? What were his reasons for choosing this profession?*

Chapter 8

- *Why did Mr. Jarndyce insist that Richard and Ada break up?*
- *What was Richard's reaction to this?*

Chapter 9

- *Who was Esther's mother? How did Esther know about her mother?*
- *What did Esther's mother's letter say?*

Chapter 10

- *What was Richard's opinion on the lawsuit?*
- *Why was Esther worried about this opinion?*

Chapter 11

- *What secret did Esther discuss with her guardian? Why did she do this?*
- *What was Mr. Jarndyce's advice to Esther? Do you think it was good advice?*

Chapter 12

- *What was in the letter that Mr. Jarndyce wrote to Esther?*
- *Describe Esther's reaction when she read the letter.*

Chapter 13

- *Why did Esther think that Richard's home was unhygienic?*
- *Why did Ada refuse to go home with Esther? What secret was revealed to Esther?*

Chapter 14

- *What was special about Mr. Woodcourt's Yorkshire appointment according to Mr. Jarndyce?*
- *What did Ada reveal to Esther at the end of this chapter?*

Chapter 15

- *Why did Mr. Woodcourt escort Esther home? Explain in detail.*
- *What proposal did Mr. Woodcourt make to Esther? What was her reply?*

Chapter 16

- *Why didn't Esther have the courage to see anyone that night?*
- *In brief, describe the conversation Esther had with her guardian after breakfast.*

Chapter 17

- *Who summoned Esther to Yorkshire and why?*
- *Why did Mr. Jarndyce cancel his marriage plans with Esther? Do you think he was right to do so?*

Chapter 18

- *What did Richard tell Esther when she arrived to see him?*
- *Describe the events that led to Richard's death from the court.*